†HE CUCA RACHA

GARRY SOMERS

ILLUSTRATED BY JACQUELYN BRIGGS

Published by **The Blotter Magazine,** Inc.

Text copyright 2013 by Garrison Somers

Illustrations copyright 2013 by Jacquelyn Briggs

First Printing 2014

This is a work of fiction.

Any similarity or resemblance to persons living or dead is merely coincidental.

ISBN: 978-0-9839022-32

Published in the United States by Lightfinger Books, an imprint of The Blotter Magazine, Inc. 1010 Hale Street, Durham, NC 27705.

Printed and bound in the USA.

The Cucaracha

Garry Somers
Illustrated by Jacquelyn Briggs

Dedicated to my girls - Kristin, Liv and Bea.

GS

The First Baptist was an imposing concrete edifice that harkened back to the days when soldiers in colorful uniforms with gold piping and impractically tall hats draped with braid might march directly into hot cannon with all sorts of pomp, prepared heart and soul to meet their maker that very morning or afternoon. And although there currently weren't any, it certainly appeared possible that someone might petition the congregation to add matching parapets and archer's slots to match "the moat," the church's wheelchair access ramp. This ramp required the physically challenged to park in the back by the church's kitchen entrance, ascend by arm strength only to the back corner, carry on along the entire block-long length of the building, turn the front corner and continue up half its width in order to finally arrive at the narthex doors. Elderly members of the congregation who used walkers or Jazzy chairs usually preferred instead to lean on stronger arms and privately reflect on the sin of pride while negotiating the blisteringly white limestone front stairs extending out from the church like a corrugated and petrified tongue razzing the entire town. "Haa-HAA! Stand in awe! I am the biggest house of worship in the county!" jeered that tongue attached to the mouth of the church. And while this may have been true enough, and despite its look of stalwart castle and keep, the First Baptist also had its share of insidious problems, one of which was that certain ladies of the church didn't play well together. No, not well at all.

*****

One morning just a little bit ago, a man squatted in a small alcove off of said church's kitchen, scratching with a pencil on a scrap of printer paper filled on the flip-side with first draft sermon. Assistant Pastor Klightus was an unfortunately named man, and he had turned his frustrations with that and his weak chin and limp hair and the smattering of ridiculous juvenile freckles that framed his nose, and all of the other painful aspects of his life inward. Although he regarded this action as reflection on the Lord's word, it was in fact merely what the young kids in the local high school's Computer Programming and Web Design class called a "do-loop", repetition of a process with no beginning or end. Less than useless, because it wasted what could, if applied to someone else, be called valuable time. Klightus was not the lead pastor at First Baptist, and he was not permitted to provide the homily at the eleven o-clock service, nor lead the choir, nor visit important (that is, of course, rich) members of "our extended church community" as Pastor Johnson – he who was Lead Pastor – liked to call the congregation when they attended to the bumps and bruises of life in the local hospital.

No, no, somewhat-less-Reverend Klightus was assigned to what he considered must be the most mundane details of a going concern like First Baptist – the kitchen and the nursery. If there was a Hell, and Klightus believed with his whole mind and heart that indeed there was, then he deemed this assignation as a kind of pre-hell. Punishment, perhaps, for something as petty and arcane as the Lead Pastor's disapproval of how he, Klightus, drank his coffee. Early on in his ministry here, Klightus had been seen by the senior pastor assembling his cup and sugar and cream – Klightus preferred to lighten his drink with real Heavy Cream and three heaping spoonfuls of sugar – and Pastor Johnson had said with great humor, "Good drippin' chicken gravy, Brother Klightus. You'll never grow hair on your chest with that concoction." This exclamation right in front of Mrs. Wiggins the gospel organist and Mrs. Plant, the head secretary, who everyone knew was an awful snitch. Klightus thought it was an inappropriate thing to say, and the two women had giggled at the words, even as everyone patted Brother Klightus on the shoulder in what might otherwise have been interpreted as friendliness. What

was it that had set off Pastor Johnson –
the sugar? The cream? Didn't they drink
mothered coffee in Texas? Or was it that
Pastor Johnson thought Klightus was a
putz? Or was it perhaps because Klightus
was lettered, a Doctor of Divinity, while
Johnson had a mere Baccalaureate with
Seminary and two years in Vietnam
during the war as a *Battlefield Chaplain*.
Envy had been the root of many an evil,
the thin, admittedly wispy and actually
hairless-chested minister reflected.
But, no. Klightus shook his head for the
umpteenth time that morning. He knew
the real reason.

His office wasn't even on the
administration hallway with the other
pastors and secretaries. As if in Roman
purgatory, Klightus had a small desk and
a phone in an alcove off the kitchen,
supposedly for his convenience. He
was certain that it had been a pantry in
some earlier church iteration, although
no one would admit this to his face.
The phone was an old sky-blue Princess
style, probably picked up from a yard
sale. There was no room on the desk

for a personal computer, and so Klightus had not been provided with one. What he was given was a ledger book to track grocery receipts for the infinite number of absolutely insipid pancake breakfasts, and a weekly nursery attendance sheet which he had to take to a secretary because the copier had a page-counter security feature and he did not have the four digit code to run his own copies. He'd silently refused to ask for the code, and no one had bothered to offer to reveal it to him. In his mind it was just one more insolent act by the hired help.

And he'd been planning to get his own personal computer – Dell was having another sale on low-end laptops – but he didn't have enough savings to do that and also get his Cressida repaired. The Toyota's air conditioning was not working. It would start and run for a moment as he backed out of the parking space in front of his apartment, but by the time he got to the stop sign the compressor would kick off and that was no good for summers in East Texas. Good Lord, Klightus hated sweating. His best white undershirts were stained yellow under the arms, where the chemicals in the deodorant he used had permanently bonded with his own... humors...no matter what he used to launder them. The car had to be fixed, he mused with a bitter smile at his play on words. So although it was too bad about missing the sale, maybe this fall he'd buy the computer, he kept meticulous, albeit temporary, records of his ministry in journal form; on sermon print outs rescued from the recycling trash, or on the backs of old stapled copies of Christmas carols he'd found stored in a closet in the nursery. One of these days he was going to give that closet a good spring cleaning. It was a junk-pile of half-burned tapers, food-crusted Cherub Choir blouses and even a rusty Menorah, the presence for which he could find no explanation. Exhausted at the idea of that much work, Klightus put down his pencil, sat in his chair in his alcove and prayed his do-loop prayer until the phone rang.

*****

Texas State Senator's Wife Eleanor Piffle's Lincoln Continental tooled west-northwest along I20 from Dallas. TSSW (she thought of herself by this acronymic matronimic whenever she thought about herself, which was often and well) Eleanor Piffle was a contented soul. She puffed at a Virginia Slim and exhaled towards the window, open like a postal letter slot to draw away the diaphanous air. Daddy - she called her husband the state senator Daddy - was staying in the city tonight; that was alright, as an elected official he did that from time to time. Eleanor preferred their home in Garrison; it was prettier than Dallas, and all hers. Their house was big, only a tad less fabulous than those owned by oil people, and lavishly ornamented in stone and iron and cedar and slate. Yes, she was nearly content.

Nevertheless, Eleanor had to admit, she was not completely *happy*, and frequently noticed that distinction. Her life in town, as a TSSW, made her peacock-proud. Her connections, those associations that she joined or led or directed in town, gave her the recognition she deserved. But there was one niggling issue.

Her pride and joy was her garden. Eleanor worked tirelessly on her yard. Not herself, of course, not actually toiling on her knees in the dirt, but her gardeners, the two Aztecs that worked the magic of her fertile imagination. Her efforts were on paper, with colored pencils. Design was one of her strengths, the ability to think of things that weren't yet there, and communicate with simpler people so that they understood what she required. It was a talent she had, a gift that she gave to the people in town who drove past her beautiful house and saw her lovely garden.

Texas State Senator's Wife Eleanor Piffle sighed. What a fetid pack of lies. She was neither happy nor content. Not even accommodating and compromising. She struggled in her heart, because the smile she wore was a sham, the pride in her life was false. Yes, there was one thing that State Senator's Wife Eleanor Piffle hated – but which she could never, ever admit – and that was Texas itself. The very place she lived. Sometimes she sat in her parlor office, off of the intimate family dining room, and vented her displeasure. She was a local girl, but hated it. She didn't like Texas cities, and the distances between them – not far enough to fly but too far to comfortably drive. She hated the hard weather, cruel winters and blistering summers, and the home-towny, just-folksy people that never changed. She hated that her escape was impossible, because her husband loved Texas to no end. Daddy had no aspirations to become Congressman or Senator Piffle in Washington – just *representing* Texas, only visiting Texas to get re-elected or on holi-days like one might a distant unpleasant but filthy-rich relation.

"Oh, sweet-tater, we'd have to spend all that time back East," he told her. "I just couldn't do that to you." And she never told him Yes! Yes! Back East! That would be fan double-damn tastic! Instead they drove to Dallas, or down to Austin and back to Garrison or Kilgore or

Longview to meet with other politicians or businessmen or constituents. And TSSW Piffle fed and watered her hatred like she might have her garden, if she cared directly for her garden at all, which she didn't.

She particularly loathed that there were copies of the high school yearbook in the local library. She had tried to have them removed, in her role as Member of the Library Board of Directors, to no avail.

"We have limited shelf space, and there are many fine works of literature that we need to make available to our town," she argued in that gentle voice she used when she wanted her way. She pronounced the word "litter-a-tour", so that she might seem above the others socially. So that she appeared originally from out of town, with refinement and education the likes of which they could only dream. But none of the others on the Board was aware of the real reason she wanted the yearbooks gone, so inadvertently her argument started a groundswell of support to add on a wing to the library. She had to support the move, because everyone believed that it was her idea, and so she took frustrated credit, and pledged a substantial amount of Daddy's money to fund the project.

"Damn and double-damn," was what she really thought. For inside one of the yearbooks that she couldn't throw out — her junior year at High — was a picture. Full page, black and white, of her and that woman. That double-damned Margarita Flor.

Once upon a time, they'd been fast friends. Ellie and Margie. They weren't cheerleaders, but they were the next best things. Twirlers. In the absolute eye-of-the-storm heyday of Baton Twirling. Ellie and Margie led every parade, took center field every half-time, and off the field they were as thick as thieves. What one girl knew, the other knew. High-toss. High-toss with a spin. Back-neck multiples. Hula catch. Their routines were flawless. In town, they were even more famous than the quarterback, who went on to Austin to suffer third string with Darrell Royal's

'Horns. There was even a dessert treat named after them down at the Dairy Queen for one summer, involving cherry ice cream, Seven-Up and two stirrers, which, thank God above, was never too popular.

Nevertheless, Eleanor Piffle, Texas State Senator's Wife, groaned to herself in recollection as she took the Kilgore exit off I-20, remembering the very moment that things went wrong.

Their senior year, Margarita Flor had learned how to twirl burning batons. Suddenly, just like that, Margie was a solo at half-time. Eleanor couldn't learn the trick; she had a fear of flames. Her Mother had brought that on.

"One spark from that baton and your hair will go up in flames like Atlanta, darlin'. Final Net is unforgiving."

Ellie pleaded with her mother to be able to go back to the pony-tail of her younger days.

"Those California hippies wear ponytails, Eleanor," her mother replied quietly and matter of factly in that coercive manner that Ellie later fashioned for herself. The discussion was ended. Ellie certainly didn't want to be a hippie.

It was a cold war, hers and Margarita's, and like the other one it was all the rage. Everyone loved to watch the struggle between two queen bees buzzing in the same cramped hive. Margarita led the homecoming parade with her burning sticks and Eleanor had the lead in the Autumn musical. Margarita went out with the toughest, most beautiful of the car-boys; those hoods who hung out in the auto-shop. He was greasy and muscled and looked like, and could very well have been, if he'd had one, Elvis's little brother. Eleanor sought retaliation by dating, in succession, an addle-pated captain of the football team, the pimply-faced captain of the basketball team, the inches-too short captain of the baseball team, and the Class Valedictorian. That particular and peculiar lad - who bypassed Harvard altogether and went to work with Jet Propulsion Laboratories directly after high school graduation - never overcame the night that Eleanor let him touch her "second base". The

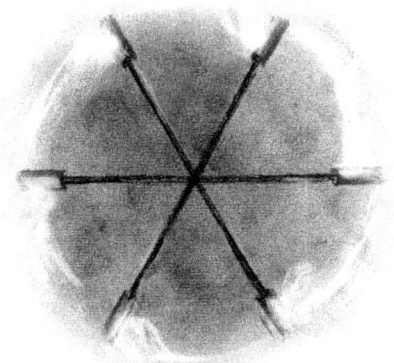

boy was so smitten with Eleanor that he named various projects after her, like the Eleanor Search for Meaningful Extra Terrestrial Life and the Miss Piffle Solid Fuel Module. Graduation looked to settle things, for a while, at least. Eleanor was taking her mother's advice and going to Baylor to become a nurse, while Margarita prepared to go off to West Texas U to do the same.

"Our brave boys in Viet-Nam deserve the best care," Graduate Eleanor explained to her satellites - already looking for other stars to orbit. Still frustrated, she ignored a letter from Margarita saying that before they scattered to the four winds, they should at least talk. But rumors of a faulty prophylactic in the back seat of a rebuilt fifty-three Ford changed the tie into a victory, and her father drove her off to school two days before a pregnant Margarita got married, with Eleanor feeling smug and brave and hopeful about the future.

Swimmingly was how she thought the next dozen years went. Victory was never sweeter. Nursing school, her tour in Tokyo – she never made it to Saigon – meeting Daedelus "Daddy" Piffle, who was a Lieutenant in the US Navy assigned to Hospital Ship Administration. The two young lovers loved being overseas - Japan was just made for American servicemen and women in love. Eleanor was in heaven. With the blessing of their parents, they were married. Then, inexplicably, Daddy didn't want to stay in the Navy, and so they returned home. Still, Eleanor had to admit to herself, with LBJ in the White House, it surely was a fine time to be in Texas. The World was

Texas, and vice-versa. Daddy became a businessman. Though there were better opportunities outside the borders of The World, he went to Neiman-Marcus and sold them on his management skills. They got a nice apartment in Dallas. Within six years, he was a director of finance. They discussed their plans - the world was an oyster and all that. Their investments were gushing money. But, Daddy preached, the power was in serving the people. So they moved back to Garrison. It was high time to conquer local politics. Councilman. Board of Education. State Congress in Austin. Was his darling Eleanor ready to move to the capitol?

"We need to have a home base, Daddy," she had told him. Gratefully, he built her this beautiful house.

Indisputable proof that there was a God in the Heavens was in knowing that Margarita lived with her plumber husband on the other side of town in a matchbox ranch with a redneck trampoline in the side-yard and grand-children romping around trampling the lawn and breaking off the blooms. Evidence that He didn't always think the same way as Eleanor was Margarita's friendship with Shirley Bird. Eleanor Piffle spent valuable time and good money making her garden the show-spot in the county, something for everyone else in town to covet. But Shirley Bird was a god-blessed gardener. And every year since nine-teen-seventy-nine, Shirley Bird's compact little plot had won the Garrison Botanical Society's annual award for best overall home garden. *Damn and double-damn again!*

TSSW Eleanor Piffle turned the Continental into her driveway and the brass glory of her second-place garden. She hated it, and now she was done with it. She yanked out her cell phone and dialed.

*****

Shirley Bird dragged the rocking chair behind her. It was, she'd long ago decided, one of those miracles of the age, this rocker. Aluminum, plastic and canvas, it was made somewhere in the land of those industrious Chinese, and sold at what the great-grands called "Wall-Mark" for change back from a twenty. You could fold it up and tote it along, or fling it in the back of the car to take to the catfish place for a picnic lunch. Strong enough to bear the weight of her fat old bum, it was just shy of perfect for sitting in the garden and watering, or leaning forward to pluck the straw-grass or bulldog that infiltrated when she wasn't looking.

What a beautiful day, she thought. She had peonies that were about to burst into bloom, following the azaleas, which she had plucked so that they weren't wearing the tattered widow's weeds of faded flowering.

Maybe tomorrow morning, she estimated, and leaned back on the rocker to stretch out her back and to take a suck on the water bottle, which she had filled with cool red Delaware Punch poured from a can. She looked up. The mockingbird that lived in the top of the cedar tree was imitating everything that had ever crossed its path. Mack, her late husband, loved mockingbirds.

You never get bored around them, he always said. Mama Mocks teach their babies the songs they learned from their mamas, he'd told her. When you hear a mockingbird, you're hearing the history of birdsong. Mack had liked to go around with the hedge clippers, pretending to beautify, while she worked on her flowers, bent over, her dairy-air pointed up for him to admire while the mockingbird sang its tunes, occasionally swooping down at his ball-capped head, trying to chase him out of what it thought was its yard. She missed Mack, a lot. She'd made this garden beautiful for him. He was a big, good, gentle man and they had loved each other quite a bit. He liked her winning awards so that he could brag on her down at the menswear store where he was a salesman, or after church services at the coffee urn in the fellowship hall. She missed him awful.

Her back was tolerable today, but her knees were a mess. *At eighty-eight, let's see your legs,* she thought to herself with a sigh. There were days when she looked down and saw them as two anchors made of some nightmare baloney. Chop them off! Because they wouldn't obey her and carry her weight or stop paining her? Selfish. Other days, she was content with concluding that she was an old mama-dog and life had pains and so it goes. This was one of those days. Because it was Wednesday and that meant Evening Service over at the First, and tonight she would be rocking.

Search for joys, she thought, leaning over a hillock of phlox and hunting for potato bugs that would clan together like Visigoths and nibble through an entire spring bloom if you didn't stop them. Find joys and hold them close. Her children were away East and the grands were married now and busy getting their own lives going. There were even greatgrands and she had pictures all over the Frigidaire and framed on the dresser and the bedside table: spring dresses and Easter bonnets and splashing at the pool and in *Star Wars* costumes where, it was carefully explained to her, one was "Loop" and the other was "Dark Tomato" and they carried "lifesavers". It made no sense and she didn't care. She wished they would visit more often. They were some of her joys. Mack's garden was another.

Rocking on Wednesday Evenings was the third joy. Five old lady rockers and Shirley was the oldest. Five rocking chairs, pretty new ones that replaced the old flat-cushion-bottom oak chairs that had been there since before Shirley could remember. The new chairs were gliders, and soft and she liked to rock to where she was almost asleep with a baby in her arms. The nursery was carpeted and smelled like talcum. The baby in her arms invariably smelt like baby: warm and sour and tinkly and precious.

She dwelled on babies and Mack and Peonies and then it was time for lunch — purple-hull peas with warmed up brisket and sliced tomatoes smeared with Hellman's. With a smile, Shirley recalled how much Mack loved simple lunches. She left the rocker out in the yard and slowly made her way back inside. She ate while watching her stories on the television and took a nap

right in her chair until her legs woke her up. Slowly, carefully, Shirley took a bath and got ready for church. Pulling on her sweater, the phone rang.

*****

Pastor Klightus felt a tingle in his nethers as he talked on the phone. Partly it was that his butt was asleep from sitting in this old wooden chair, but mostly it was that Mrs. Piffle was the only member of the congregation that called him by his first name. Pastor Klightus sounded like an affliction requiring painfully inserted medication. Pastor Bill sounded less formal, more shirt-sleeve, down in the dirt of evangelism, friendly and involved. *Good old Pastor Bill. He's a heck of a good preacher, aint he? Golly Moses, he sure is.*

"I'm not one to pass along bad news," Mrs. Piffle said. "But it's a question of safety. And there's no matter more important than the safety of our children is there, Pastor Bill?"

Klightus shook his head, then remembered that he was on the phone, no one could see him shaking his head. *Maybe she can hear the rattle,* the negative voice inside his head criticized.

"Safety is important," he said. He was frequently at a loss for words, a terrible affliction for a preacher, even one that didn't preach. He countered it by repeating what the person said in a positive way, something he had learned from a pamphlet called "Effective Listening" he'd found in the nursery closet.

"She's one of our eldest members. Perhaps it is time for her to retire."

"It may be time for her to retire," Pastor Klightus said, with a smile — because while you couldn't see a head shaking, you could hear a smile in a phone conversation.

"I'm glad you see this so clearly, Pastor Bill." TSSW Eleanor Piffle said.

Klightus beamed. Then a cloud crossed his horizon. He was hesitant even to mention it.

"But what if she doesn't want to retire? There is no mandatory retirement age for volunteer workers at the church." It was true, Klightus thought.

"Then you will need to find a way to make her want to retire, Pastor Bill," Mrs. Piffle said. Her tone had changed, like a cloud changes an afternoon sky. Even though she'd said his first name again, there was no smile in her voice, which had taken on the threatening edge of a rusty blade. "She is a hazard and, of course, the wellbeing of the nursery's young occupants is your responsibility. You should handle this."

Klightus nodded again absent mindedly before saying,

"I should handle this."

"Right," she said with smiling warmth. "You know, this is precisely the way for you to move up that old ladder. Handling responsibility, I mean."

"I should handle this," he repeated. He heard Mrs. Piffle sigh on the other end.

"You might tell her that she deserves more respect in our church. Let her know that she should be permitted more rest, and that it was irresponsible of our church congregation to continue to make her chase after children in the nursery. We should have been taking better care of her needs, but she has been doing such a fine job that no one was doing theirs. You take it on the chin, Pastor Bill, for the team. You apologize to Miz Shirley. Then you could tell her that she doesn't have to come all the way out to the church on Wednesdays just to work, but now she can sit and relax and worship. Or even stay home on Wednesdays, if she wants to. Tell her that either way she doesn't have to worry about it any more. You'll get someone to step up to the responsibility, because it's her turn to take a break. Got it?"

Pastor Klightus wished that he

had thought to take notes on the back of a Christmas Carol. His armpits weren't just damp. They were draining water like a faucet.

He hated sweating.

"Got it," he said.

Mrs. Piffle hung up without saying goodbye, which was her standard method of ending telephone calls. Klightus stood in his chair and massaged his behind, which was still tingling and numb. *Crapdoodle,* he said to himself. *I have to fire Miz Shirley Bird.* He mulled it over and over and over again. Like so many of his burdens, it didn't go away. He picked up the phone.

*****

Shirley sat in her kitchen, which was warm and homey-smelling. She'd been boiling purple-hull beans for her after-church supper, but she'd turned off the stove when the phone rang. Now the pot sat on the table, where it was probably peeling the finish on the linoleum. She sat with a hot-mitt on her hand. Shirley didn't know what to do. She was dressed for church. If she was going to go, she would have to do her face again, because she had been crying. Shirley didn't really want to go anymore, wasn't sure what to do next, because she thought she might not be finished crying, either.

Brother Klightus had rung her up right as she was ready to head out. She liked to go early, and tidy up the nursery before service.

"Miz Bird, how are you doing?" he said.

"I am fine," she said. She hadn't recognized his voice, so had said nothing more. There was a long pause as the phone line crackled. Finally he broke the silence.

"This is Pastor Klightus, down at First Baptist," he said.

"Oh," Shirley said. One word came into her mind, and she was not proud of it. *Frig.* That was what her Mack would have called Klightus. A frig. A useless, pencil-necked, knuckle-dragging, slack-jawed frig. A lesser portion of a man. She pushed this from her mind. "How are you, Brother Klightus?"

"Well, Miz Bird, I am just fine this afternoon." Klightus smiled broadly, so that she would hear it in his voice. His jaw cracked under the weight of the lie.

"How can I help you," Shirley asked. She was in a hurry, and it would take time to park and walk her paining legs up the long handicapped ramp to the door of the church and then back down to the nursery.

"Miz Bird, it's how I can help you," Klightus said, and he began his oily, smarmy spiel.

Shirley loved rocking the babies. It was a perfect joy. She told Klightus this and he kept on telling her that it was work. She was entitled to some rest, he reminded her. She was a respected elder in the congregation and had done her part for the church and other people should now do the work she was doing. Maybe he was right. She was old, and God knew that she couldn't forgive herself if she dropped one of her sweet babies.

She let a few more tears fall. *Oh, frig.*

*****

Margarita Flor-Collins drove as if she had taken lessons with Dale Junior. *Damned lights,* she thought. A couple of her turns were fancy, with stone-spittin' fishtails and everything. It was her husband Randy's pickup truck, which he didn't particularly appreciate her driving, and she'd surely told him what-was-what about that. Randy was a big man, but he understood what side of his bread the butter was on and he shut up about it right quick.

No one had seen Shirley that evening, and no one had gotten a call from her. Her best friend, Lorelei had driven by her house that morning, honked when she saw her in the yard.

"She waved back. I would have stopped, but I had ice cream in the back, and we had just talked the day before and I knew I would see her tonight," Lorelei fretted. "I should have stopped."

"It's alright, Miz Lorelei," Margarita gently patted the older woman on her deeply curved back.

"You know, she still drives, sometimes," Lorelei said. "She won't give up Mack's old LTD." Margarita hadn't known that.

"How does she see over the dashboard?" she asked.

"Yellow Pages," Lorelei said. "Two copies. She sits on them. One for each cheek." Margarita grinned in spite of her worrying.

"I'm going over there directly." And she barreled off across town.

*****

"He said what?" Margarita said again.

Margarita's latte-colored skin was ruddy with the fine blossom of her outrage. She and Shirley were old pals. Shirley knew that she didn't need to repeat anything. Margarita had arrived sweatily terrified that Shirley had fallen, broken a hip or collar bone or something. Couldn't get up and call. She'd knocked repeatedly on the door, calling Shirley by name, before the she heard the familiar fiddling with the lock to open the door. Margarita set right into her. Shirley, you had everyone so worried. Yes, I can see you're OK, but then why hadn't you gone to church tonight? Were you ill? Margarita looked questioningly at Shirley's eyes. Shirley told her.

Margarita's friends sometimes referred to her as a *hot-shit*. In any other world, that might have been taken wrong, as an insult of some ilk, even a smack-the-crap-out-of-you insult, but everyone who knew Margarita agreed, she was indeed a *hot-shit*. She was closing on sixty years old, and looked and seemed like she was in her mid-forties, tops. She had young friends and old friends, and ferocious energy and loved life in a way that smoothed away any ravages of sun and age and gravity. Her children were grown with children of their own, but she was not the typical sedate grandmotherly type, and her kids and grandkids loved her for it. They all lived in town, choosing happily to stay in her orbit rather than spinning off into the cosmos. After almost forty years, her husband, Randy adored her. He often just sat back and let her run wild, occasionally coming by him for a kiss and a pat on the fanny before taking off again with renewed vigor. Her original plans for a nursing career, gently blunted by her marriage and children, had eventually picked up steam after the kids had grown. Randy had given her a good old-fashioned kick-in-the-pants towards the junior college in Tyler and after many miles of driving, many late hours trying to make her old brain absorb what used to come so easily in her youth, moving on to courses offered on computer and at the local hospital, she had received her nursing degree. She wasn't an RN, her dream of so many years earlier, but being an LPN had fulfilled her in ways she wouldn't have imagined as a hungry teenager.

She saw Shirley twice a week, and massaged the elderly woman's legs, making sure that nothing was worse than her previous visit. They talked, and Shirley made coffee or tea, and baked up biscuits and they ate and sipped, talking about husbands and gardens and Texas and how some things changed over time, but some things didn't. Margarita had become one more person-link in the chain of folks in the town and surrounding environs who checked on people like Shirley. They asked after each other, and visited and ran errands for one another. If one person was going to Wal-Mart, or the Eckerd store, they might call over to see if maybe Shirley, or Miz Mapletree, or retired Doc Jackson needed anything. *Oh, it's no trouble. Yes, ma'am, I wrote it down, the six ounce bottle, not the eight ounce. Yes, they are dear, aren't they? Well, you gotta take them, or it swells right up, doesn't it? I'll be right over after I fetch them. See you soon.* And so on. And if you ran into someone standing in line to check out, you talked with them. *How are you? How is Adelaide? How is Old Mr. Portage? Yes I heard about his stomach. He won that cake at Church in a raffle, and was afraid that it would go bad before he ate it all. My grandson couldn't eat a whole cake in three days, much less that foolish old man. Yes, he's sitting on the bench for Baylor, and happy to do it.* And so on. Everyone knew how everyone else was. It was a good system.

"Who in the name of all that's holy does he think he is?" Margarita simmered. She had a glass of iced tea in her hand, and was certain that the heat running through her was melting the ice unnaturally fast.

"He's the nursery pastor," Shirley said softly. Her eyes were red from tears, but she hadn't cried in front of her friend. Crying was a private thing.

"He's not the boss of anyone," Margarita said.

"Oh, I know," said Shirley. She was embarrassed now, and puttered around in the kitchen to cover it. "Well, I guess I'm retired."

Margarita swallowed her anger. It banked in her gut like a fire.

"No, Shirley," she said firmly. "You like rocking those babies. You are good with them and everybody knows it."

The older woman shook her head, feeling sorry for herself.

"No, he's a *frig* but he's right. I'm old and I might drop a baby. I can't sit down and get up so good when I got a baby in my arms. It's dangerous."

"That's crap, Miz Shirley, if you'll pardon me," Margarita said behind gritting teeth.

Shirley turned on a burner to heat up some more water, although there was already a full pitcher of tea on the table. She was flustered and unhappy and wouldn't be turned from this line of thinking, so Margarita shut up and drank her tea. She asked her friend about today's stories and Shirley wound down and sat on her chair and the two talked about As The Supper Burns.

Damn and double-damn, thought Margarita, when she climbed back in Randy's pick-up. It ain't right. And it wasn't going to do. If she had to, Margarita was going to blast Pastor Klightus a brand new one.

*****

"Members of the congregation have spoken frequently about her commitment and dedication," Pastor Klightus said. He was in the corner of his tiny office, sitting on his chair, with his back against the wall, literally and figuratively. Truth be told, Margarita Flor-Collins terrified him. Most *women of color*, as he referred to them, scared him somewhat, but Margarita was tough and smart and didn't look her age, which meant that she had hidden wisdom. That added to his fear that she was unpredictable and therefore unmanageable. And smarter than he.

Not to mention the secret. *The Secret.*

Not so way back when, Pastor Klightus had been assigned to First Baptist with great expectations. He was fresh from completion of his doctorate and this was going to be his first flock. No, he wouldn't be the lead pastor, but with his newly acquired theological knowledge he could only expect to leap swiftly into important and relevant roles in this large church. Except that Klightus had trouble with people.

It couldn't be just his fault that every time he had to interface with members of the congregation, they seemed to be the weirdos and difficult cases. He was assigned to building and grounds maintenance and evening bible studies. All of the building and grounds employees were Mexican and he didn't always understand what they were trying to tell him. There were members of the congregation that wanted to maintain the gardens themselves, rather than letting the Mexicans do it. And every blessed Sunday like the devil's own clockwork someone was complaining about the length of the church's wheelchair ramp. And of course the bible studies were under-attended. People preferred to meet in each other's homes, without a pastor's oversight. Klightus might have been able to work out the bugs in these assignments, except that bright one Sunday morn a number of members of the congregation came to early service only to find that one of the men's restrooms was inexplicably fouled with vomitus. That week Pastor Johnson called on Pastor Klightus.

"Bill, I don't want you to consider this a demotion. There's no such thing as a demotion in this church, just new opportunities," Pastor Johnson said in his rumbling baritone voice, famous for its capacity to throw a mighty sermon to the far edges of the sanctuary and onto the airwaves; Sunday services were broadcast on AM One Oh One Three. "What I'm mostly concerned about is that dirty laundry was aired. We always check on Saturday night and again on Sunday morning that our Rock (he proudly and consistently referred to the First Baptist Church edifice as the Rock) is as immaculate as the mother of Christ herself." Klightus imagined that Pastor Johnson wasn't so concerned that high school boys had snuck in from Youth Ministry to chug down most of the communal wine stores as he was that the vomit bespattered hoppers and sinks irrevocably proved that it had happened. And so the lowliest assistant pastor had been re-assigned to cover the nursery and kitchen maintenance, never imagining that there were tasks ranked lower than vomit-patrol.

Klightus had been frustrated by the meeting with Pastor Johnson, and was moping in his alcove when Mrs. Margarita Flor-Collins had come into the kitchen, to put some leftover raspberry Danish in the fridge.

"Good morning, Pastor. How's every little thing?" Margarita asked.

She looked in his face, saw that he was troubled, and pulled up a chair. In a few minutes of intense conversation, she pried his problems out of him. What resulted was worse than the problem.

"You'll like her. She's nice and friendly and funny," Margarita told Pastor Klightus. She had him convinced that what he needed was to get out, meet people, and have a life beyond his responsibilities to the church. Margarita even knew a girl that he should meet. It could be a lunch date, no pressure. Not even a double date; Margarita would come with a couple of girlfriends, so that it would be the four of them. A low key introduction, she called it. But I promise, she's very friendly, Margarita reiterated. She clapped him on the shoulder and went on her way. Klightus felt the miserable dampness under his arms.

The day of the get-together arrived and Klightus went to the diner. He got a table for four and Margarita arrived alone. In spite of his trepidation, he was surprisingly crestfallen.

"No, they're coming on their own," and she grinned at him for being so jumpy. "Don't worry, you can't lose on this one." She gave him a sly elbow in the ribs.

The girls arrived. They were attractive women, Klightus had to admit, and younger than Margarita. He had been worried that he would be meeting a woman old enough to be, well, his older sister. He popped to his feet for the introductions. Margarita waved her hands.

"Rhonda, this is Bill Klightus," she said. The taller of the two women smiled broadly at him. He stuck out his hand.

"Hi! I'm Pastor Bill," he chirped. As he watched, her smile faded to a polite hello. Margarita stared at him for a second before recovering. Nevertheless, he recognized the brief look. It was *What were you thinking? You were on your way, pal-o-mine, when you sent that particular locomotive careening off of the tracks.* He knew exactly what she meant by her freighted look, although he wouldn't say it, even subvocally. He knew because he'd seen the look before: not everyone wants to "date" ministers.

Klightus never pulled it back together that evening. His hands shook, he couldn't figure out where to look, so he found himself flitting his eyes about the room like a wounded pigeon. His armpits were like faucets, and his breath went sour on him, no matter how much water he thought he surreptitiously swished around in his mouth. Everyone was polite, but only just so. He had crashed hard and burned long.

"Ok then. We'll just keep that one between us," Margarita said later in the week, when she came across Klightus in the hallway outside the nursery. She mixed her metaphors for him, saying that they were first at-bat jitters and he needed to get back on the horse. Margarita convinced Klightus that she could arrange a dinner date. Rhonda had liked him well enough, she said. No mention of the "P" title, no backwards collars, no long blessings before chowing down. So he had gone on the second date, meeting Rhonda at the unfortunately named Mission Steak House, in the strip-mall near Interstate-20. And even though

Rhonda had done most of the talking, as Margarita had suggested, the date had nevertheless fizzled.

"Bill, did you ask her if she attended church?" Margarita quizzed him after.

"No, I swear I didn't," he said.

"Did you go anywhere after dinner?" she asked.

"No," he said quickly. But glancing in her eyes, he saw something there. Insight.

Because Margarita already knew better. Klightus had gone with Rhonda back to his apartment. For coffee, she said. And Rhonda admitted to Margarita that she had gone along because although the young man had seemed so confused, well...sexually, still she had liked him. *I mean, You know,* she told Margarita, *how sometimes it becomes a challenge? But,* she explained to Margarita, *nothing doing. Guess he must really swing that way, even if he can't get a grip on it just yet.* She had used every trick in the book. Margarita nodded, waving her hand. She didn't want the details on what every trick in the book meant to her young friend, Rhonda.

Margarita didn't reveal all of this to Klightus. What he didn't know was exactly what she did know. And it didn't matter. A mystery was as damning as any truth in a small town like Garrison.

"We'll keep this one to ourselves, as well," she shrugged like someone holding a hot hand. He had nodded, relieved, for he had known what she meant, or thought he did. And so she had kept The Secret.

But today she was going to beat him upside the head with it.

*****

"Who fires a volunteer?" Margarita asked Pastor Klightus. They sat in the kitchen near the sinks. The doors were closed. She answered her own question. "Nobody. And especially you don't fire Shirley Bird. For double-pity-damned-sake, Pastor, she's eighty-freaking-nine." She seemed to be leaning over him as she talked, although they were both standing and both the same height.

Pastor Klightus tried to muster up the will to resist the bulldozing he was getting.

"Members of the congregation have voiced a concern," he started.

"God, Bill, that's just so much crap," Margarita said, turning and smacking her forehead. Had they been outside, she might have spit in disgust.

Klightus felt his shoulders going up. Margarita snapped a look that stopped him cold in mid-shrug.

"You don't do this to people." She was breathing hard. Her anger was getting the best of her. Klightus felt the beginnings of his life passing before his eyes. There was a lameness and bland quality to it.

"Come on. Who voiced concerns?" the woman insisted.

"I can't say," Pastor Klightus said, mistakenly relaxing an iota.

Margarita subdued an urge to twist off one of the little frig's spaghetti arms.

"There is no such thing as the sanctity of the confessional in the Baptist

Church, you imbecile," Margarita fumed. "One secret kept is another spoken."

Klightus wilted. If she was already calling him names, pain could only follow directly.

"Eleano..." he started, but she cut him off like the honed, hacking blade of a machete.

"That bitch." Margarita's eyes went black with anger, like a shark's. Taking a deep breath, she explained to the associate pastor what was going to happen, and what he had to do, or she would turn her real and righteous anger loose on him.

"Oh, my." And for the first time in his life, Klightus was truly moved to pray. He followed the urge.

*****

The forty-years-in-the-making cat-fight began on a Friday evening. One of Margarita's husband Randy's roles as plumber was overseeing the occasional contracted emptying of residential septic tanks in the area. He had a regular pumper that he used, the Winsted twins, Clyde and Pearl, a brother and sister act working the high-wire of human fecal matter and gray-water removal. They weren't local, choosing instead to live near Kilgore and do the work over in Garrison, for reasons that only a septic pumper could explain.

"Yes," Margarita said.

"No way, Margie. No," Randy replied, but he looked at his wife and knew that he wouldn't get his way on this one. He'd seen Margarita ticked-off before, but not like now. And part of him was curious to see what would go down, like watching a nature show on TV: a wildebeest and a crocodile in the same bit of muddy river.

"She wasn't even trying to hurt Shirley," Margarita squeezed her fists on the table. "She was trying to get at me. She's just too chicken-salad to come at me directly." Randy nodded solemnly. But Margie needed to cool off. He told her so – just because it was the right thing to say, not because he actually expected her to. Only then should she go speak to Eleanor Piffle. Semi-concerned, he double checked to make sure that the gun safe was locked up while Margarita stalked around the house unloading the whole story on him, the heels of her bare feet fairly sending sparks off the oak floor. She wouldn't drive over and shoot Eleanor, he reasoned, but she just might take a shot at the TSSW's Lincoln Continental.

"That's what we're going to do," she said. "Call them."

Randy rang the Winsteds. Clyde answered. Randy asked the pertinent question.

"Yes, about eight hundred pounds worth of effluent, a quarter tank or so. We could ditch it, but it's not yet worth the trip." Then Randy told in two sentences what Margie had taken an angry half-hour to explain.

"You want us to do what?" Clyde put Pearl on the other phone. Sometimes she was better at figuring things. Yeah, she wants to get Piffle for getting Klightus to fire Bird.

"Well, OK," his sister said, grasping the situation immediately. "OK. Yeah, I can do that. Right, we'll meet you there."

48

So, Clyde thought, we're off.

"You can't pour stuff all over Eleanor Piffle's lawn, Margarita," Randy said softly. He had learned in the fullness of time that you can't argue loud with Margarita. She always won that one.

"Oh, honey. I don't plan to," she said. There was a smile starting to cross her face, a little devil of a smile. Oh, boy, he thought.

Within the hour, Margarita met Pearl down the street from Eleanor's house. It was dark now.

"Everything working?" she asked mysteriously.

Pearl was out of the truck already. She gave a thumbs-up.

"Easy, squeezy," she said. "After you empty a tank, you can go back and there's always a heck of a lot of the little buggers. We just pumped them up."

"You're going to get us in trouble," Clyde said, shaking his head. Saying it didn't change anything. Knowing that Pearl and Margarita were friends, there was nothing he could do to stop this. Anyway, Randy always referred them for services. Clyde was nothing if not loyal.

"No, we'll be fine. You have enough hose?" Margarita asked.

"Oh, hell yes," Pearl said. She began reeling it off onto the street.

"Let's go. We have to move before a squad car comes by," Margarita said. If Officer Keifer came and asked what they were doing, he would never let them finish. He wouldn't arrest them, would maybe even laugh, but would never let them do it.

Pearl pulled the hose down the street. It was about twice as wide as garden hose, and heavy, but Pearl had biceps like a defensive back, stringy and strong. They reached the corner of Eleanor Piffle's yard. There was a fence-wall combination here extending over to the driveway. They would have to move quickly to get to the front door. Margarita grabbed the hose with one hand and helped Pearl.

Up the steps of the front porch, all concrete and stone, the two women stepped with their burden. The movement sensitive porch chandelier burst into brilliant light. Pearl set down

the hose and backed away, into the
bushes below. She pulled a walkie-talkie
from her jeans pocket and tapped on
the call-button twice, their signal for the
guys to start the pump.

"Here we go," Pearl said. She was
a tough looking broad, but her giggle was
childlike and silly.

Margarita rang the doorbell and
stood there, as compressed air built
up in the containment vat on the truck
and the cargo rumbled down the long
black hose. As Eleanor answered the
chimes of her front door, the first shit-
besmeared cockroaches shot from the
end of the hose like pellets from an
ungodly shotgun. Dozens, then many
hundreds of the crawling insects scooted
in the open door of Eleanor's palatial
home. Their black and brown bodies
were counterpoint to her lemony-white
tile floor and her creamy carpeting. Ellie
saw Margie standing there, under the
porch light, arms crossed, face taught,
as her own feet coated with awful offal-
odored cock-roaches that were crawling
energetically into her beautiful home.

Texas State Senator's Wife Eleanor Piffle screamed. Loudly, and a lot. She jumped with a fervor that she hadn't possessed since high school. She aged two or three years. She fought back her gorge, again and again with the skill of an experienced registered nurse. She avoided tinkling down her leg in horror, but only just. It was quite a moment. She grabbed for her door to slam it against the tide of cockroaches, missed, and spun to the ground. Now the roaches were crawling on her, in her lap, up her skirt.

"I! Aye!" Eleanor tried to say I'll kill you for this, but couldn't put the sentence together. It was OK, though. Margarita got the message.

"I don't think you will. I think you will stop thinking about yourself all of the time, and sit down and start being a good girl, Ellie," Margarita said quietly. "Or else."

In the beastly insanity of the moment, Eleanor still had the presence of mind to admit that last kind of froze her. Margarita turned, tapping her shoes so that any cockroaches fell off onto Eleanor's welcome mat.

The hose was already reeling madly back down towards the truck. Pearl had snuck away quietly, to a place where she could see things but not be seen. And, it seemed, that no one else had seen anything, either, for Eleanor Piffle's front door was sufficiently far enough away from her neighbors that they hadn't heard her scream. Or perhaps they did and didn't care. Unfortunately, all that was lost on Eleanor.

And she was never provided with an explanation for Margarita's prank. A pest-removal company van drove up to Eleanor's house the following morning, unbidden, to assist with her cockroach problem. It parked right in front of the house, for the whole town to see, and its crew took all morning spraying and crawling around under the house searching for the infestation. Eleanor made plans to join Daddy in Austin the following week. "I just miss you," she lied.

But the Wednesday after that, TSSW Eleanor Piffle was well aware that Shirley Bird was back in church, rocking babies from her glider. As offhandedly as she was able, Eleanor asked one of the secretaries, who told her that Pastor Klightus had assigned a high-school student (and paid her twenty-five dollars a week) to hand the babies to Shirley and take them from her loving arms when she was done, so that the old woman didn't have to get up to do it herself. Eleanor peered through the one-way glass in the nursery door. There was Shirley, rocking back and forth with a child in her arms, eyes closed, smiling. *I'll be damned,* Eleanor Piffle thought in wonder. She made a mental note to call Klightus, but every time she tried to work up her own righteous anger, she felt the tickle of little insect feet instead.

Jacquelyn Briggs earned her BA in Studio Art with a Minor in English from Appalachian State University in 2010. She has worked as a freelance illustrator, cover designer, exhibiting artist, and painting teacher. Presently she is living in London where she is studying for an MA in Illustration at the University of the Arts London. Her goals are to continue working in freelance illustration and as an independent artist, and to continue her education so that she has enough experience to support a career in a variety of artistic fields and pursuits.

Garrison Somers is editor of The Blotter Magazine in Durham, NC. Lightfinger Books (an imprint of The Blotter Magazine, Inc.) are intended for use by folks sitting in waiting readers usually would prefer not to be where they are. Often, there isn't much to do to pass the time and take their minds off of those things that concern them most. We hope that these books help even a little bit with that very thing. If you would like to make a small donation to help offset production costs of this and other Lightfinger Books, check us out on www.blotterrag.com.

We hope you enjoyed reading yet another micro-novel brought to you by Lightfinger Books.

Collect 'em all & share with your friends.

For more information, to see our other shenanigans, or to make a donation to our cause, visit us at
www.blotterrag.com

¡Ay, caramba!